"Only by encouraging individual freedom, or the individual power of the mind, and by trusting our own feelings, can collective acts be meaningful."

AI WEIWEI

For my children

N.R.

For all brave people with big ears

G.D.

Originally published in French as *Au-delà de la forêt* by Nadine Robert and Gérard DuBois copyright © 2016 Comme des géants, Varennes, QC, Canada
English translation copyright © 2021 by Greystone Books
This edition was published by arrangement with The Picture Book Agency, France.
All rights reserved.
First published in English in Canada, the U.S, and the U.K. by Greystone Books in 2021

21 22 23 24 25   5 4 3 2 1

Greystone Kids / Greystone Books Ltd.
greystonebooks.com

Cataloguing data available from Library and Archives Canada
ISBN 978-1-77164-796-0 (cloth)
ISBN 978-1-77164-797-7 (epub)

Editing by Kallie George
Copy editing by James Penco
Proofreading by Alison Strobel

Jacket and English text design by Sara Gillingham Studio
Jacket illustration by Gérard DuBois

Printed and bound in Malaysia on ancient-forest-friendly paper by Tien Wah Press

FSC
www.fsc.org

MIX
Paper from responsible sources
FSC® C012700

Greystone Books gratefully acknowledges the Musqueam, Squamish, and Tsleil-Waututh peoples on whose land our office is located.

Greystone Books thanks the Canada Council for the Arts, the British Columbia Arts Council, the Province of British Columbia through the Book Publishing Tax Credit, and the Government of Canada for supporting our publishing activities.

Canada

Canada Council
for the Arts

Conseil des arts
du Canada

BRITISH COLUMBIA

BRITISH COLUMBIA
ARTS COUNCIL
An agency of the Province of British Columbia

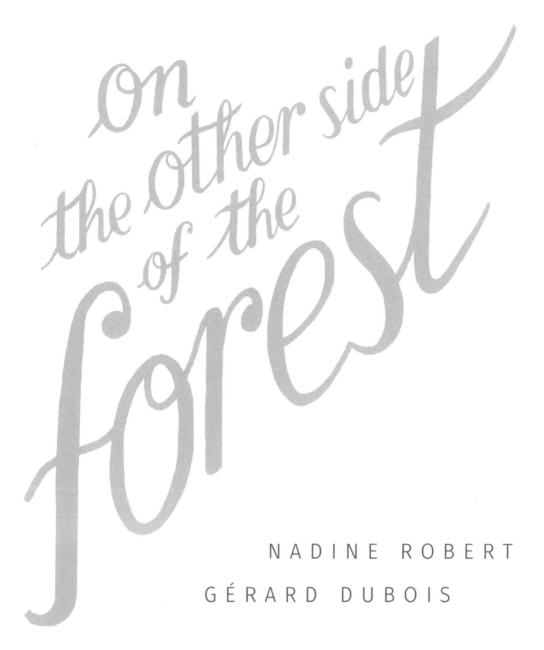

On the other side of the forest

NADINE ROBERT

GÉRARD DUBOIS

TRANSLATED BY

PAULA AYER

GREYSTONE KIDS
GREYSTONE BOOKS • VANCOUVER/BERKELEY

I live with my dad and my dog, Danton,
on a little farm, in the middle of a clearing
surrounded by a big forest.

People say that wolves live in the forest,
and ogres, and giant badgers.

No one ever goes in there!

My dad isn't the sort who believes these stories.
Still, the forest is too dense and dark to go through.

And he's always wanted to know what's on the other side.

Dad usually whistles or hums a tune while he works.
But today, he's quiet and deep in thought.

When he's tying his last bundle of wheat, he shouts,
"Arthur, I've got it! I've just had a magnificent idea!"

"We're going to build a tower," he tells me. "A very tall tower
so we can see over the trees to the other side of the forest!"

"A tower?" I reply.

"But what are we going to build it with?"

"Let's go to the mill and grind this grain," says Dad,
loading up the cart. "I'll explain to you on the way."

As soon as we get home, Dad puts his plan into action.
With the flour that we've milled from the grain, he makes some dough.

Then, he shapes dozens of round loaves,
working late into the night.

When I wake up, our house is filled with the smell of toasty bread.

The delicious smell attracts Mr. Bobbin, our neighbor,
who's walking along the path.

"I'd like to buy a loaf from you," he says.

"I'd be happy to exchange one for four large stones," Dad replies.

"Stones? For a loaf of bread?" Mr. Bobbin says, surprised.
"Very well. I'll be back soon!"

Mr. Bobbin returns, followed by several villagers
who are also carrying stones.

Soon the loaves have all been traded for stones.

"Time to get to work, Arthur!" Dad says.

We build until lunch.

While Dad naps to regain his strength, I play with Danton.

We'll need a lot more stones to make our tower high enough.

Dad wakes up when the sun goes down.
He makes us some dinner, then goes right back to his baking.

"I can't believe it! My idea is working," he says.

Early in the morning, the smell of bread fills the clearing again.
I wake up to the noise of the villagers coming up the road,
with their wheelbarrows and carts full of stones.

"What are you doing with all these stones?" Mr. Bobbin asks.

"We're building a tower!" Dad explains.

"So we can see what's on the other side of the forest."

Just like yesterday, when the bread is all gone,

we go back to building.

It's very tiring. But a magnificent idea
takes a lot of work.

When four o'clock chimes, Dad goes inside to mix the flour, water, and yeast. Then he's so tired, he falls asleep!

To help him, I finish making the dough and I clean the oven.

When Dad wakes up, the dough is ready.
"You did a great job, Arthur!" he says, and I smile.

This time, we add some nuts, cheese,
and olives to our loaves before we bake them.

When the sun comes up, even more villagers than yesterday
are waiting in front of our house, with even more stones.

Our tower is getting tall.

"Soon we'll be able to see to the other side of the forest!"
Dad says excitedly, wiping his forehead.

But at the end of the day, the sky darkens.
Big black clouds are approaching.

Danton whimpers when the thunder roars.

After the storm, the villagers are there as usual with their stones.
But we have no bread. And the tower is ruined.

Dad, asleep under a tarp, doesn't move.
He's completely exhausted.

Then . . .

. . . something MAGNIFICENT happens!

"Dad, Dad! Wake up!
The tower is twice as tall as before the storm!"

My dad can't believe his eyes.

He goes straight to the kitchen without a word.

By the time the villagers head home, the loaves are ready.
"How could we thank you otherwise?" he says.

The next morning, all the villagers come back with stones,
and their tools too. Dad gives directions as they stack the stones.
We all work as hard as we can.

The tower rises and rises, higher and higher!
Before the sun sets, I curl up under a tree, my dreams filled
with visions of what might be on the other side of the forest.

I'm not sure how long I sleep,
but when I open my eyes, the tower stands before me.

It's . . . magnificent!

That evening, before we climb the tower for the first time,
everyone from the village joins us to celebrate.

Dad can't contain his joy! Neither can Danton.
The tower is done!

I can't wait to get to the top!
Dad and Danton and I climb as fast as we can
while the villagers cheer us on.

We reach the top, panting for breath, and at last we can see
what's on the other side of the forest.

the end